Penny
the Pony
Fairy

For Emelia Macmichael
with lots of love

Special thanks to Sue Mongredien

No part of this work may be reproduced, stored in a retrieval system,
or transmitted in any form or by any means, electronic, mechanical,
photocopying, recording, or otherwise, without written permission
of the publisher. For information regarding permission, write to Rainbow
Magic Limited c/o HIT Entertainment, 830 South Greenville
Avenue, Allen, TX 75002-3320.

ISBN-10: 0-545-04190-2
ISBN-13: 978-0-545-04190-4

12 11 10 9 8 7 6   11 12 13 14/0

Printed in the U.S.A.   40

First Scholastic printing, July 2008

Penny the Pony Fairy

by Daisy Meadows

SCHOLASTIC INC.

New York Toronto London Auckland
Sydney Mexico City New Delhi Hong Kong

The Fairyland Palace

Wetherbury Village

Strawberry Farm

The Spring Show

Bramble
Stables

Jack Frost's
Ice Castle

Jane Dillon's House

The Park

Kirsty's
House

Jamie
Cooper's
House

The
Wainwrights'
House

Fairies with their pets I see
and yet no pet has chosen me!
So I will get some of my own
to share my perfect frosty home.

This spell I cast, its aim is clear:
To bring the magic pets straight here.
The Pet Fairies soon will see
their seven pets living with me!

Contents

A Pony Ride

"Let's go, Jet!" Kirsty Tate shook the reins and Jet, the black pony she was riding, set off along the forest trail. She grinned over at her best friend, Rachel Walker, who was sitting on a chestnut mare named Annie. The two girls had come to Bramble Stables for a fun afternoon pony ride. "This is the perfect

day for riding," Kirsty said happily,
feeling the warm sun on her face.

"And the perfect way to end our visit
together," Rachel agreed.

The girls exchanged a secret smile.
Rachel had been staying with Kirsty's

family during school break, and they'd had an exciting time helping the fairies of Fairyland! Jack Frost had stolen all of the Pet Fairies' magical pets. He was angry because, in Fairyland, pets choose their owners themselves. No pet had ever chosen Jack Frost! In a rage, he had taken the Pet Fairies' magic pets to his ice castle.

Luckily, the clever pets had managed to escape. But they then got lost in the human world! Rachel and Kirsty had spent their vacation rescuing the pets before Jack Frost's sneaky goblins could capture them again. So far, the girls had found six of the seven missing pets.

"We still need to find Penny the Pony Fairy's pet pony," Kirsty said thoughtfully. "I really hope we can

rescue her before you have to go home, Rachel."

Rachel nodded. "Well, we're definitely in the right place to spot her," she said. "This is pony heaven!"

Bramble Stables was located right on the edge of the beautiful Green Wood Forest.

As the ponies ambled along the path,  the girls could smell the fresh scent of pine trees, and hear birds singing high in the branches. One of the stablehands, Jessica, was leading the ride. Behind her rode another little girl and

two boys. Kirsty and Rachel were at the
back of the group. They guided their
ponies next to each other and chatted as
they trotted along.

After a few minutes, the trail took the
riders past a large pond with a few white
geese bobbing on its surface.

"Those are snow geese," Jessica called to the group. "See their black wing tips?"

Kirsty gazed at the geese as they drifted along on the water. Just then, a sudden movement caught her eye. "Look, there's a rabbit," she said, pointing it out as it scuttled behind a bush.

"Oh, and there's a squirrel up in that

tree!" Rachel added.
She showed Kirsty
where it was
perched on a
branch, watching
the horses go by
with bright eyes.

Suddenly,
Kirsty spotted a
flash of green
disappearing in the
trees. "What's that?"
she murmured,
peering through
the leaves. But
then she gasped.
"Oh, Rachel,
look," she whispered.
"It's a goblin!"

Rachel could see one of Jack Frost's
goblins peeking out from behind a tree.
Then she noticed that there
was another one sitting
high up on a
branch!

"If the goblins
are here, they
must think Penny's
magic pony is nearby,"
Rachel said. A determined
look crossed her face. "And
if she is, we have to find her
before they do!"

Kirsty nodded, and the
girls rode on. Both kept
a close lookout for more
goblins and the magic pony.

Suddenly, a few loud *bangs* that sounded like fireworks echoed through the air. The ponies at the front of the group neighed in fear and reared up. Jessica controlled her horse expertly, but the riders behind her panicked as their ponies bolted. They didn't know what to do!

Kirsty's pony, Jet, whinnied nervously and broke into a gallop. Rachel's pony, Annie, followed close behind.

"Stay calm!" Jessica shouted to the group. "And hold on tight!"

Rachel and Kirsty clung onto the reins as their ponies galloped along the path. "Do you think the goblins caused that noise?" Rachel called over to Kirsty.

"I don't know," Kirsty called back, "but whatever it was, these ponies are really spooked!"

The ponies thundered on, and the girls could see that the trail forked up ahead.

The ponies in front of them swerved down the right-hand trail without breaking their stride. Just as Jet and Annie approached the fork, two goblins suddenly popped out from behind some bushes. They set off two more loud *bangs*!

The noise scared Jet and Annie. The two ponies bolted down the left-hand trail.

"Oh no!" Kirsty cried. "Now we're going in the wrong direction!"

Magic in the Meadow

Rachel did everything she could think of to soothe her frightened pony. "It's all right, Annie," she said. "Don't worry!"

She was trying to sound calm, but she couldn't help feeling scared. The ponies were racing along at breakneck speed now, and Rachel had to concentrate hard to keep her balance in the saddle.

Don't panic! she told herself, sitting
down into the saddle and pulling back
steadily on the reins. She glanced over at
Kirsty to see her friend doing the same
thing. At last, both of the ponies slowed
down. Moments later, both girls brought
their ponies to a complete stop in a
clearing.

"Phew!" Kirsty gasped shakily, sliding
off Jet's back.
"That was
exciting."
"But scary,
too," Rachel
confessed,
slipping down
from Annie's
back and giving

her a reassuring pat. "Good girl, Annie."

Kirsty gazed around the pretty green meadow. "I wonder where we are. Do you think the ponies will know the way back to the stables?"

But Rachel was only half-listening. Out of the corner of her eye, she'd spotted something glittering on the other side of the clearing. It looked like fairy magic! "Kirsty, look!" she said,  pointing, but the glitter vanished before she could say anything else.

Rachel rubbed her eyes and stared hard, but everything looked perfectly normal now. "I'm sure I saw something magical," she told Kirsty, quickly tying Annie's reins to a nearby tree. "Let's take a closer look."

Kirsty tethered Jet next to Annie and 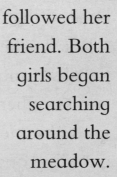 followed her friend. Both girls began searching around the meadow.

Then it was Kirsty's turn to spot something — a glimmer of fairy dust near some rocks!

"Rachel, over here!" she called, crouching down to see where the fairy dust was coming from. And then she smiled. "Oh, Rachel!" she whispered.

"Come and see. She's so sweet!"

Rachel knelt down next to Kirsty and smiled, too. There, shyly poking her head out from underneath a dandelion, was a tiny, white, sparkling pony. "This must be Penny's magic pony!" Rachel breathed. "She's *really* cute!"

"Hello, little pony," Kirsty said in a soft voice, stroking the pony's tiny

17

nose gently with one finger. "Can you help us, please? Our ponies were scared by Jack Frost's goblins. They ran and ran, and we got separated from our group. Now we're lost!"

The magic pony gave a tiny whinny, as if she understood exactly what Kirsty had said. She trotted toward Jet and Annie. Then, in a flash of fairy magic, she became a full-sized pony with the brightest, whitest coat the girls had ever seen. The pony touched noses with Jet and Annie.

A stream of silvery fairy dust swirled around all three ponies. Jet and Annie seemed to calm down at once.

Rachel grinned at Kirsty. "Fairy pet magic to the rescue again!" she said happily.

The magic pony whinnied a second time and nodded her head toward a path that led out of the clearing. She trotted that way, then turned back and whinnied again.

"She's showing us the way out," Kirsty guessed. "Come on, Jet." She untied Jet from the tree, took his reins and patted his glossy black coat. "Are you all right now, boy? Is it OK if I climb up onto your back again?"

Jet nuzzled Kirsty's shoulder and nickered softly. "I'll take that as a yes," Kirsty said, putting her foot into the stirrup.

But before she could pull herself up into the saddle, Rachel grabbed Kirsty's arm.

"I can hear voices!" Rachel whispered.

Kirsty stood still, listening. "You're right. Someone's coming," she hissed. "It's the goblins! Quick — hide!"

12

Hiding the Ponies

Rachel looked around quickly. "Where?" She gulped. The clearing was surrounded by trees, but none of them were big enough to hide the girls and all three ponies.

Before Kirsty could reply, both girls heard a voice behind them exclaim, "Glitter! You're safe!"

Kirsty and Rachel turned around quickly to see a squirrel scampering down a nearby tree. Penny the Pony Fairy rode on his back! The little fairy fluttered off the squirrel's back and thanked him politely. Then she happily flew over to her pony.

Penny had long, golden hair that tumbled past her shoulders. She wore purple knee-high boots, jeans, and a pretty purple-and-white shirt.

"Thank you for finding Glitter!" Penny cried happily, landing on her pony's nose and kissing her.

"Hello, Penny," Kirsty said in a low voice. "Unfortunately, the goblins will find her, too, if we don't get out of here quickly. They're coming this way!"

"And there's nowhere to hide!" Rachel added. She glanced over her shoulder. The goblins' voices were getting louder. Rachel was sure she could hear their footsteps now. They were sure to spot Glitter at any moment!

Penny quickly waved her
wand over the nearest
tree, a tall oak. As the
silvery fairy dust
from Penny's wand
swirled around it,
the oak became
a weeping
willow, with
long, leafy
branches.

"Perfect!" Kirsty
grinned, quickly
leading Jet under the
willow tree. "It's a
great hiding place!"

Rachel led Annie under the
tree, too, and Glitter and Penny
followed — just in time. The girls held

26

their breath as they heard the goblins coming closer and closer. "We scared them good with our party poppers!" one goblin boasted. "That magic pony is sure to come now," another one jeered. "Don't those magic pets always come to help frightened animals in the human world?"

"Well, let's hope it gets here soon," a third goblin said. "This is our last chance to get a pet for Jack Frost. If it goes wrong again, we're all going to be in big trouble!"

Very carefully, Kirsty peeked through the willow branches. She could see that some of the goblins were holding party poppers. One goblin even had colorful paper streamers dangling over his big green ears!

"I can't wait to get my hands on that pony," the first goblin said, grinning.

"It doesn't stand a chance with all seven of us after it!" another goblin chuckled.

Then the goblins started arguing loudly about which of them would get to ride the magic pony first. Kirsty, Rachel, and Penny exchanged worried glances.

"We have to get Glitter away from here," Rachel whispered to Penny. "Maybe now would be a good time, while they're all arguing?"

29

Penny nodded. "If you and Kirsty ride Jet and Annie, I'll ask Glitter to lead us back to the trail," she said in a tiny fairy whisper.

Kirsty and Rachel quietly swung themselves back into their saddles. Penny fluttered up to one of Glitter's ears and whispered into it. Glitter nodded, and when they were all ready to go, she stepped silently out from under the willow tree and away from where the goblins were arguing. Rachel held her breath as Annie pushed her nose through the willow fronds. She edged

out of their hiding place, and Jet
followed. The ponies were silent. They
seemed to know instinctively that
they had to be quiet to protect Glitter.

But then, just as Kirsty was thinking
that they might escape, Jet stepped on a
dry twig. It snapped with a loud *crack*!

"What was that?" shouted one of the
goblins. "Is somebody
there?"

All the goblins
turned toward
the girls. "Oh!
The magic
pony — it's right
here!" cheered a
goblin, hopping
from one foot to
the other in glee.

"Run, Glitter!" Penny urged. Glitter broke into a gallop and fled from the goblins. Jet and Annie followed close behind, with Kristy and Rachel on their backs.

"After them!" bellowed the goblins, charging toward the ponies.

"Come on, Jet!" Kirsty said, crouching low over his neck as he and Annie raced after Glitter. The trees were a blur as the ponies galloped through the forest. Then they were on the trail! Kirsty felt her spirits rise. There was no way the goblins would be able to keep up with the ponies at this pace.

"We lost them!" Rachel cheered after a few minutes. "Great job, Annie. We did it!"

"We must be near the end of the trail by now," Kirsty said, as the ponies slowed to a trot again. "Maybe we'll come out near the stable yard soon."

"Can you imagine Jessica's face if we rode back in there with Glitter and a bunch of goblins?" Rachel laughed.

Kirsty was about to laugh, too, but then she looked up ahead. There, blocking the path — and looking furious — was Jack Frost himself!

An Icy Escape

Kirsty gasped as Jet reared up. Annie neighed in fear and backed away.

Jack Frost just gave a horrible cackle and chanted a spell. A rope of ice snaked through the air and looped itself around Glitter's neck.

Jack Frost laughed triumphantly and

pulled the pony toward him. "Now you'll be my pet!" he declared.

"No!" cried Penny, waving her wand desperately. A stream of silvery fairy dust whirled all around Glitter. Kirsty and Rachel watched hopefully. But Jack Frost's magic was too powerful for Penny, and her fairy dust fizzled out uselessly around Glitter's hooves.

"Oh, yes," smirked Jack Frost, as he leaped onto Glitter's back. "Your new name is Icicle," he told the little pony. "And you're all mine now. Let's go!"

The girls stared in horror as Jack Frost rode away on poor Glitter's back.

"Penny, why don't you ride in my pocket?" Kirsty suggested. "Come on, Rachel, we have to try and catch up with Glitter!"

The little fairy dove gratefully into Kirsty's shirt pocket. Kirsty could feel her there, quivering with fear, as the ponies galloped after their new friend.

To Rachel's surprise, they seemed to be catching up to Glitter faster than she'd expected. "I think Glitter's trying to hang back," she said to Kirsty. "I'm sure she's not galloping as fast as she can!"

Penny had a smile on her face as she peeked out of Kirsty's pocket. "You're right," she told Rachel. "Clever Glitter — she wants us to catch up with her!"

Jack Frost rode past the sign that pointed back to the stables and headed off down the trail. By now the girls' ponies were closing in on him. Jack Frost was just about to ride past the pond when he glanced over his shoulder, and saw the girls right on his tail.

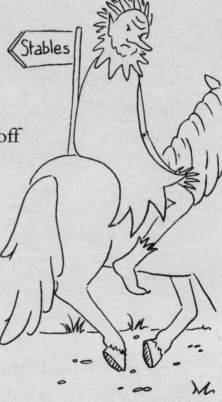

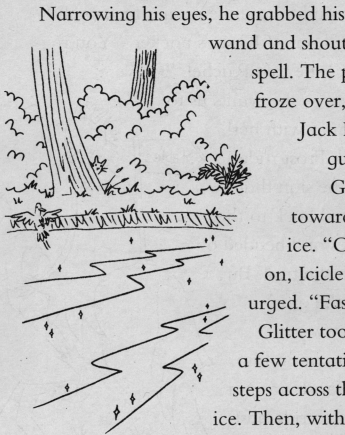

Narrowing his eyes, he grabbed his
wand and shouted a
spell. The pond
froze over, and
Jack Frost
guided
Glitter
toward the
ice. "Come
on, Icicle!" he
urged. "Faster!"
Glitter took
a few tentative
steps across the
ice. Then, with a
wicked smile, Jack
Frost leaned back and waved his wand
over the icy stretch she'd just

passed. Instantly, that part of the ice
melted back to water.

"He's making it impossible for us to
follow him across the pond!" Kirsty
realized. "We'll have to go around,
instead."

"But we can't," Rachel said. "There's
no path. We'll have to —" She broke off

suddenly as a flock of snow geese flew overhead. They swooped down toward the far side of the pond.

The girls and Penny watched as the biggest snow goose landed first, not far from Jack Frost and Glitter. The goose pecked at the ice, looking confused, and then gave an annoyed *honk*. The other

geese honked, too, as they realized their pond was frozen.

As soon as she heard the honking, Glitter pricked her ears up. She refused to go any closer to the noisy geese. Jack Frost climbed down and tried to pull her along the ice with his rope, but the little pony stood her ground. She wouldn't take another step.

"Good job, geese! They stopped Jack Frost in his tracks," Rachel said. Then a thought struck her. "And I have a great idea!"

Feathered Friends

"Maybe if Penny turns us into fairies, Kirsty, we could all fly over to the geese," Rachel said, her words tumbling out in excitement. "And maybe they can help us rescue Glitter!"

"Great idea!" Penny said.

Rachel and Kirsty quickly tethered their ponies to a nearby tree. Penny

waved her wand again and used her
magic to change them both into fairies.
"And here's some extra fairy magic, so
that the geese will understand what
you're saying," she said, sprinkling more
fairy dust over the girls.

The geese were still making a lot
of noise as the three friends flew
toward them.

"He did this!" Rachel called out to them, pointing at Jack Frost. "He froze your pond!"

Every goose's head turned in Jack Frost's direction. The biggest snow goose wagged her tail feathers and honked loudly at the others. Then they all waddled over to Jack Frost. These geese meant business! When they reached him, the geese tapped meaningfully at the ice with their beaks. Jack Frost ignored them, but they began pecking at his legs.

47

"Hey!" he shouted in surprise. "Stop that!"

But the geese didn't pay any attention to him. Soon Jack Frost was surrounded by honking, pecking, angry geese! Glitter didn't seem to like the noisy geese at all. She leaned away from them, tugging on her icy rope. Jack Frost was so busy trying to stop the geese from pecking him that the rope slipped out of his fingers. Glitter was free!

Penny flew over to the pony and

waved her wand. Fairy dust streamed out, and the rope of ice turned into sparkling snowflakes that melted on the breeze. Glitter shrank to fairy pet size again.

Penny threw her arms around the little pony. "Oh, Glitter!" she cried joyfully. "Thank goodness you're all right!"

The pony neighed softly and nuzzled Penny's hand. Penny waved her wand

and produced a juicy red apple for
Glitter.

Kirsty smiled, seeing Glitter and Penny
reunited. Then she turned to see if Jack

Frost had
noticed. He was
still trying to get
away from
the geese!
As he pushed the
biggest goose away
with his hand,
beautiful, magical
sparkles glittered
around the goose and Jack Frost.

"What's that? What's happening?"
Kirsty asked Penny.

Penny chuckled. "A pet has finally
chosen Jack Frost as its owner!" she

explained with a grin. "The snow goose wants to be Jack Frost's pet!"

"Or does she want *him* to be *her* pet?" Kirsty giggled.

On the other side of the pond, Jack Frost's goblins came crashing through the trees, but they were too late to help their master now.

Jack Frost's gaze fell upon Glitter, safe with Penny. He held up his hands in  defeat. "All right! I'll turn the ice back to water," he cried. "But you geese have to leave me alone — and stop that awful racket!" He stalked off the pond and waved his wand. The ice melted away. With a satisfied wiggling of tail feathers, the geese turned and waddled back to the pond, launching themselves into the water one by one.

"Come on," a grumpy Jack Frost called to the goblins. "Let's go home."

The goblins trailed after their master as
he stomped toward the trees.

Suddenly, with a honk of surprise,
the biggest snow goose flew after them.
She landed by Jack Frost's side, and
pushed her beak affectionately into
his hand.

"She doesn't want him to leave without her," Penny said, smiling.

"How sweet!" Kirsty exclaimed, as the goose gazed lovingly at her new owner. The other geese came out of the water, too, waddling over to join Jack Frost and the goblins.

"It's nice to have a pet," Penny
agreed, patting Glitter. "I'm glad Jack
Frost has someone to love now, too.
And I'm even more glad that I have
Glitter back," she added, smiling
at Kirsty and Rachel. "Thanks so
much, girls!"

Rachel
fluttered her
wings happily.
"Now all of the
fairy pets are
safe." She
beamed. "We
did it!"

"I'd better take
Glitter back to Fairyland,"
Penny went on. "Would you two like
to come with me?"

A smile broke over Kirsty's face. "Yes, please!" she cried eagerly. Then she looked over to where Jet and Annie were tethered. "But we should really get the ponies back to the stable," she said.

"The ponies will be fine," Penny said reassuringly. "I'll work some magic so that it seems like you're only away from them for a second."

"Hooray!" Rachel cheered. "Then we'd love to come to Fairyland!"

Perfect Pets for Everyone

Penny waved her wand and a cloud of
fairy dust billowed from the tip. It
enveloped her, the girls, and Glitter in a
whirl of sparkles. Seconds later, the girls
found themselves in Fairyland, right
outside the palace.

King Oberon and Queen Titania were

waiting in the palace gardens. All the other Pet Fairies were at their sides.

"Welcome back, Kirsty and Rachel," the queen said, smiling at them. "Thank you so much for helping our Pet Fairies."

The king stepped forward. "You did well, my dears. Once again, you have helped the fairies and brought order back to Fairyland."

Rachel and Kirsty curtseyed. "It was a

pleasure, Your Majesties," Kirsty said
politely.

"But what if Jack Frost
tries to steal our pets
again?" Bella the
Bunny Fairy asked.
"How do we know
they'll be safe?"

Penny gave her a
wink. "Don't worry,
Bella," she said. "Now that Jack
Frost has his own pet, he doesn't need to
steal anybody else's."

The queen smiled and sprinkled a little
fairy dust over the nearby pond. The
surface shimmered with magic, and
Kirsty and Rachel leaned over to look as
a picture appeared. It showed Jack Frost's
palace — with a new pond in front of it!

"That wasn't there before," Kirsty said with a grin.

"And look! There are the geese!" Rachel laughed. "They look very happy in their new home, don't they?"

The girls smiled to see Jack Frost sitting on a bench near his pond. He was feeding the largest snow goose some bread, and patting her gently. The two of them really did seem to like each other!

Katie the Kitten Fairy cuddled
Shimmer, her kitten. "The
fairy pets are definitely safe
now," she said.
"Hooray!"
Sunny the puppy
bounded over to
Rachel and gave
her a lick as if to
say thank you.
Then Sparky the
guinea pig squeaked
something.
"She says, 'Nice job,
Kirsty and Rachel',"
Georgia translated with
a grin.
"I think we all agree with
Sparky," the queen said,

giving the excited guinea pig a little smile. "But I'm afraid I must return you to your own world now, girls. Annie and Jet need you to take them back to the stables."

"They know the way," the king added. "You'll find Jessica and the others waiting there. If you hurry, you'll get back before Jessica has to ride out looking for you."

"Before you go, though, we'd like you each to have one of these," the queen said. She waved her wand, filling the air with a flurry of golden fairy dust. When the dust cleared, Kirsty and Rachel saw that they each had a new charm bracelet sparkling on their wrist. The bracelets were silver chains with seven tiny charms that shimmered with all the colors of the rainbow.

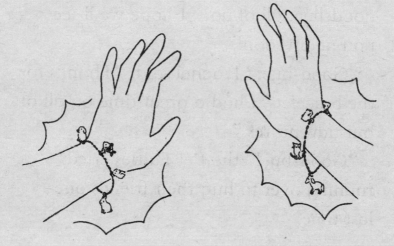

"Oh, Kirsty, look!" Rachel cried in delight. "A kitten, a rabbit, a guinea pig, a puppy, a hamster, a goldfish, and a pony!"

"You'll never forget your adventures with the Pet Fairies now," the king told them, his eyes twinkling.

Kirsty shook her head. "Never ever," she agreed. "Thank you so much. And good-bye, all of you. I hope we'll see you again soon!"

"Good-bye," Rachel said. "Thanks for the bracelets. I had a great time on all of our adventures."

"Good-bye!" the Pet Fairies cried, running over to hug their friends one last time.

Then the queen raised
her wand and waved it
over the girls. The world
seemed to spin in a
blizzard of fairy dust, and
then Rachel and Kirsty
found themselves back by
the ponies.

Kirsty untied Jet and
swung herself up onto his
back. "Let's get back to the stables like
the king told us to," she said. "With a bit
of luck, we'll still have time to go out for
one last ride with Jessica before my mom
comes to pick us up."

"Good idea," Rachel said, climbing up
onto Annie's back. Then she grinned at
Kirsty. "Race you there!"

THE FUN DAY FAIRIES

Rachel and Kirsty helped all seven Pet
Fairies, but now the Fun Day Fairies are
in trouble. Can the girls help

**Megan
the Monday
Fairy?**

Take a look at this special sneak peek!

"I'm glad I'm staying with you during vacation," Kirsty Tate told her friend, Rachel Walker, as they came out of Fashion Fun, the accessory store on Tippington's Main Street. "And I hope these sparkly clips will look good with my new haircut!"

"I'm sure they will," Rachel said cheerfully. "They're so pretty."

"Thanks," Kirsty replied. "I wonder how the fairies are," she added, lowering her voice.

The girls walked through the iron park gate and across the grass. The park was filled with colorful flowers, and in the middle was a large brass sundial shining in the light.

"The sun's bright today," Kirsty said.

Rachel nodded. Then she noticed something that made her heart beat faster — tiny golden sparkles were hovering and dancing above the sundial!

"Kirsty, look at the sundial!" Rachel gasped. "I think it's fairy magic!"